the MILO & JAZZ MYSTERIES®

11

THE CASE OF THE LOCKED BOX

by Lewis B. Montgomery
illustrated by Amy Wummer

KANE PRESS
New York

Text copyright © 2013 by Lewis B. Montgomery
Illustrations copyright © 2013 by Amy Wummer
Digital Illustration Enhancement by Mark Wummer
Super Sleuthing Strategies original illustrations copyright © 2013 by Kane Press, Inc.
Super Sleuthing Strategies original illustrations by Nadia DiMattia

Montgomery, Lewis B.
The case of the locked box / by Lewis B. Montgomery ; illustrated by Amy Wummer ;
Super Sleuthing illustrations by Nadia DiMattia.
pages cm. — (The Milo & Jazz mysteries ; #11)
Summary: When detective-in-training Jazz, accused of stealing 100 dollars from a
locked cashbox, stands trial in student court, it is up to her sleuthing partner, Milo, to
prove her innocence.
ISBN 978-1-57565-625-0 (library reinforced binding) — ISBN 978-1-57565-626-7
(pbk.) — ISBN 978-1-57565-627-4 (e-book)
[1. Trials—Fiction. 2. Stealing—Fiction. 3. Schools—Fiction. 4. Mystery and detective
stories.] I. Wummer, Amy, illustrator. II. DiMattia, Nadia, illustrator. III. Title.
PZ7.M7682Cal 2013
[Fic]—dc23
2012051086

7 9 10 8

First published in the United States of America in 2013 by Kane Press, Inc.
Printed in the United States of America

Book Design: Edward Miller

The Milo & Jazz Mysteries is a registered trademark of Kane Press, Inc.

Visit us online at **www.kanepress.com**

 Like us on Facebook
facebook.com/kanepress

 Follow us on Twitter
@KanePress

For Fiora and Marina,
who like puzzles
—L.B.M.

Titles in *The Milo & Jazz Mysteries* series:

THE CASE OF THE LOCKEd BOX

CHAPTER ONE

Milo poked a fork into the cup and stirred the crumbly brown stuff around. "There's no worm in this dirt!" he said. "Did someone eat it?"

"Don't worry, we have plenty extra." His friend Jazz dropped a gummy worm into the cup of chocolate cookie crumbs. "If we run out of anything, it'll be the sunflower seeds."

Selling "seeds and dirt" at lunchtime to raise money for the school garden was a great idea, Milo thought.

Actually, Jazz had tons of great ideas. As student council president, she seemed to come up with a new plan every day. The only problem was that it didn't leave her much time for solving cases.

Milo and Jazz were sleuths in training. They got lessons in the mail from world-famous private eye Dash Marlowe and solved real-life mysteries. But lately, Jazz had been so busy—

"Milo, did you hear me?" Jazz said.

"Huh?"

"I *said*, the principal said he'd think about my idea of having a student court. But he's worried we're too young."

Milo shrugged. "Maybe he's right. Kids aren't always fair."

"Neither are grownups!" Jazz argued. "But they have the right to a trial by jury. We should, too."

A younger boy came puffing up. "Hey, Jazz! Sorry I'm late! I folded all the paper napkins like you said."

He dropped them on the table by the metal cashbox.

Jazz gaped at the fluffy white pile. "Billy, I just wanted you to fold them in *half*. I didn't mean you had to fold them into origami!" She paused. "Um . . . what are they supposed to be?"

"Slugs!" Billy announced cheerfully. "You know, to go with the whole garden thing."

As Billy set out his napkins at the far end of the table, Milo leaned over to Jazz. "Origami *slugs*?"

"At least he's trying to be helpful!" she said. "Unlike Chelsea."

Chelsea, a fourth grader, was vice president of the student council. Billy was secretary, and Omar, a boy in Jazz's class, was treasurer.

Chelsea was always telling everyone that *she* should have been president, and that it wasn't fair only fifth graders could run for the top spot. She was jealous of Jazz and never missed a chance to cause her trouble.

"What did she do now?" Milo asked.

Jazz pointed at the cups of cookie dirt. "Yesterday she knocked one off the table accidentally and wouldn't help clean it up. She said it was *my* dumb idea to sell messy snacks. I had to crawl around under the table picking up the crumbs myself so Mr. Schiff wouldn't get mad."

Milo nodded. The school custodian could get a little grouchy about spills.

Voice rising, Jazz went on, "THEN, while I was down there cleaning up the mess, one of the teachers came by and told her what a great fundraiser it was. And guess what Chelsea said?"

"What?" Milo asked.

Jazz mimicked Chelsea's prissy tone. *"Thank you! It was my idea, you know."* She switched back to her normal voice. "Can you believe that? I was so shocked, I started to stand up under the table and

I bonked my head."

"Ouch." Milo winced.

"Anyway," Jazz said firmly, "I don't care what Chelsea says. We're earning tons of money for the garden."

"How much have you got so far?" Milo asked, eyeing the locked cashbox.

Jazz broke into a smile. "Over a hundred bucks! The box is *stuffed*."

A small key hung on a string around Jazz's neck. She slipped the string over

her head and pulled the cashbox toward her.

"Soon I'll need to trade some of those dollar bills for fives and tens," Jazz went on as she turned the key in the padlock and flipped up the lid. "Or else—"

She stopped. She stared.

Milo stared, too.

The cashbox was completely empty.

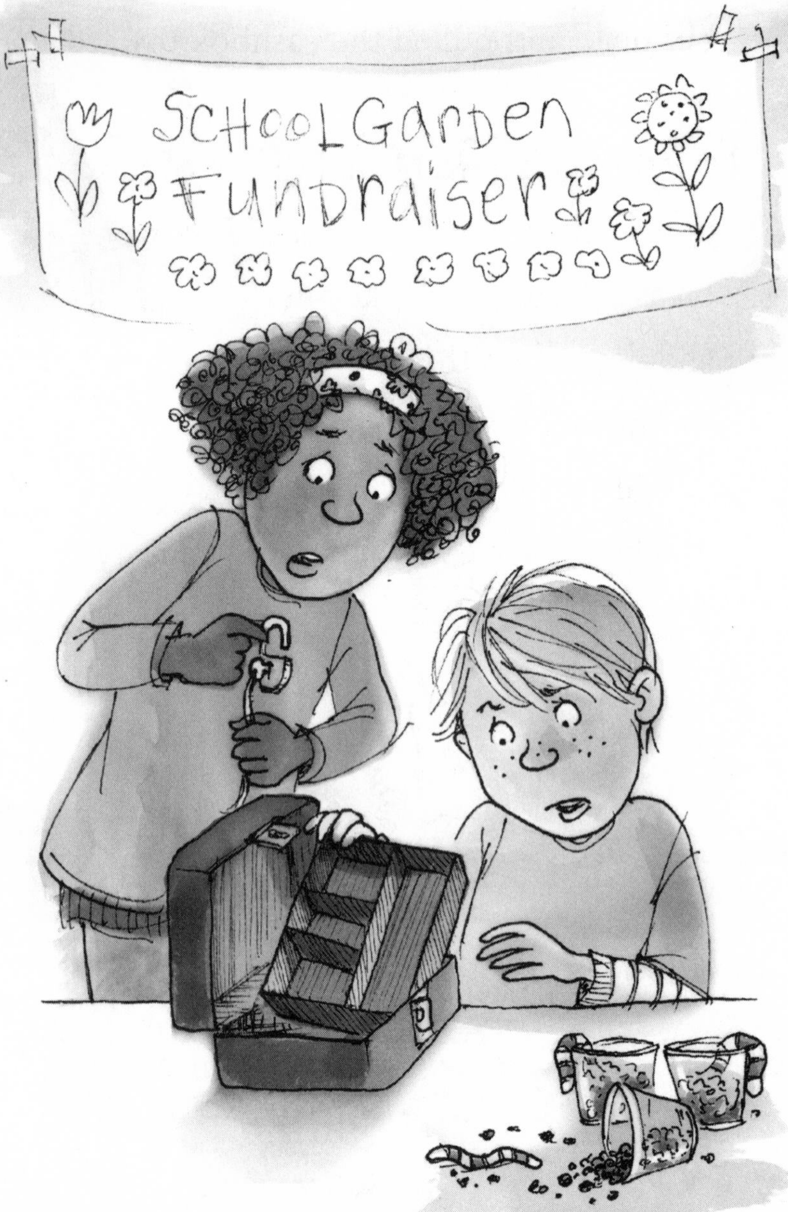
School Garden
Fundraiser

CHAPTER TWO

"The money!" Jazz exclaimed. "It's . . . it's *gone*!"

Milo lifted the black plastic tray. Nothing underneath, either. He frowned. "Probably someone took it to trade in for bigger bills. Like you were saying."

"But that's impossible!" Jazz said. "They'd need the key."

"You're the only one with a key?" he asked.

"Well, Omar has one too, because he's student council treasurer—"

"Maybe he's off counting the money, then," Milo said, looking around.

Jazz shook her head. "He hasn't been in school all week. He's been home sick. Anyway, Omar would never take the money out of the box without telling me."

Milo picked up the open padlock. "Are you sure it was locked?"

"Of course! I just unlocked it!"

Milo pulled the key out of the lock. He clicked it shut, then tugged on it. Locked. He stuck the key back in and twisted it.

The lock sprang open.

"It seems fine," he admitted.

Jazz stared into the empty cashbox as if she expected the money to appear with a *poof.*

"Maybe you put the money somewhere else and then forgot?" Milo said.

"How could I forget?" Jazz asked.

He thought. "Well . . . you said you bumped your head yesterday, right? Maybe you have amnesia."

"Milo, don't be silly." Jazz scowled. "Somebody must have stolen our school garden money. But who would do a thing like that?"

The answer came to Milo in a flash. "Chelsea!"

"What?" Jazz said.

"Chelsea stole the money!" he said. "Don't you see? Remember yesterday, how she spilled that stuff on the floor? I bet she did it on purpose, to distract you! While you were cleaning up her mess, Chelsea was cleaning out the cashbox."

Milo grinned. *Ta-da!* Even Dash Marlowe couldn't solve a case that fast.

Jazz stared back at him, wide-eyed. But then she shook her head. "The money was still there after that. I counted it before I locked the box at the end of lunch."

The air rushed out of Milo. "Oh." And it had seemed like such a perfect solution!

By now, a crowd had begun to gather. Kids clustered around the table, jostling for a closer look at the empty cashbox. Sunflower seeds spilled everywhere. Billy flung himself across the table. "Hey! Don't squish my slugs!"

The principal cut through the crowd. "What's going on here?"

"It's the garden money," Milo said. "It's disappeared!"

As Jazz explained, the principal's frown deepened. "The box was left in the school office overnight?"

Jazz nodded. "Right behind the desk. The same as always."

"Someone could have gone in when the secretary wasn't there," Milo said. "Like when she goes outside to help get kids onto the buses after school."

"But no one else at school had a *key*," Jazz reminded him. "So nobody could have gotten the money out of the box except . . ." Her voice trailed off.

"Except YOU!"

A girl in a headband pushed forward. "*You* stole the money. Didn't you?"

Jazz gasped.

The crowd buzzed.

"That's a very serious accusation, Chelsea," the principal said.

"She practically admitted it herself!" Chelsea said. "Nobody could have taken the money out of the box without a key.

And who had the key? *She* did."

Chelsea pointed a skinny finger straight at Jazz, who looked stunned.

"Student council officers should be trustworthy," Chelsea went on primly. "We don't need a thief for president."

"Hey, wait a minute!" Milo protested. "This is America. People are innocent till proven guilty, right?"

"YES!" Billy yelled. "In a COURT OF LAW!"

Everyone stared at him.

Eagerly, Billy turned to the principal. "Jazz has been saying we should try a student court, right? Well, now we can put *her* on trial!"

Jazz's mouth moved, but no sound came out.

"We can have a real judge and jury," Billy went on happily. "And lawyers—you know, the one who says you're guilty and the one who's on your side."

"Prosecution and defense," the principal said, looking thoughtful.

"Yeah!"

A wave of excitement was rising. Kids turned to their friends, chattering about trials they'd seen on TV.

Billy beamed.

"Well, Jazz," the principal said. "You

have been asking for a student court. What do you think?"

Jazz's eyes slowly scanned the crowd. Milo followed her gaze. A few kids smiled at her. Others whispered to each other, or just stared.

Turning back to the principal, Jazz stood very straight. She raised her chin. "Let's do it."

CHAPTER THREE

Everybody wanted to be at the next day's
trial, even though it meant missing recess.
All the fourth and fifth graders were
hoping to be chosen for the jury.

The principal arranged for a student
judge from the middle school to run the
trial. The middle school principal also
sent over a boxful of little booklets titled
HOW A TRIAL WORKS.

THE COURTROOM

A.

E.

F.

B. D.

C.

Milo carefully studied his booklet as he and Jazz sat in his kitchen eating an after-school snack. Jazz had picked him to defend her. He figured it was going to be a tough job—especially with Chelsea on the other side.

"Chelsea is really out to get you," he told Jazz. "And she has a pretty good case."

WHO'S WHO AT A TRIAL?

A. Judge: oversees the trial and makes sure the rules are followed

B. Defendant: the person on trial

C. Lawyer for the prosecution: tries to prove the defendant committed the crime

D. Lawyer for the defense: tries to show problems with the prosecution's case against the defendant

E. Witnesses: tell what they saw or heard relating to the crime

F. Jurors: vote the defendant "guilty" or "not guilty"

"She can't prove I stole the money when I didn't," Jazz said.

"She can tell the jury you're the only one who *could* have done it. Then the jury can decide you must be guilty. Unless . . ."

Their eyes met.

"Unless someone catches the real thief?" Jazz asked.

"I happen to know a good detective," Milo said.

"Me too!"

They grinned at each other.

Then Jazz frowned. "I just can't figure out how the thief got the money out of that locked box."

"Do you know where your key was the whole time?" Milo asked.

She pulled out the key on its string. "Right here around my neck."

"What about Omar's key?"

Jazz brightened. "Of course! I should have thought of that. Maybe he left it in his desk at school and someone took it!"

"Or maybe he got tricked into handing

it over," Milo said excitedly. "What if the thief went to Omar's house and said you lost your key and had to borrow his?"

"I'll call Omar now," Jazz said.

While she dialed Omar's number, Milo leafed through the pile of mail. There was an envelope addressed to him with *DM* in the upper left-hand corner.

"Hello?" Jazz said into the phone. "This is Jazz. May I speak to Omar?"

Milo fidgeted impatiently as Jazz waited for Omar to come to the phone. When he did, she told him what had happened and asked about his key.

Her face fell.

"Are you sure?" she said. "Oh . . . oh. Well, okay. . . . Yeah, I hope we find the money, too. Thanks, Omar."

Hanging up, she turned to Milo. "Omar says the key is home with him. He's had it the whole time."

"He's sure?" Milo said.

Jazz nodded. "He double-checked."

So much for that. Milo opened the lesson from Dash, and they bent over it together.

DASH MARLOWE

SECRETS OF A SUPER SLEUTH!

Make a Model

Even the best sleuths are rarely on the scene to see a crime take place. Figuring out what happened can be tricky, with criminals trying their best to keep you in the dark.

How to shed light on the situation? One way is to make a model (a small copy) that lets you reenact the crime and see how it could—or couldn't—have been committed.

I used this strategy when the famous British racehorse Bob's Your Uncle disappeared the day before the Royal Cup. Bob's owner called me down to the police station. There, a weeping jockey, Dodgy Della, told us she had taken Bob out for a practice trot.

"I was about to 'op on the 'orse," Della explained, "but the sun was in me eyes, so I stopped to put on me cap. That's when 'e sneaked up on me from behind."

"The horse?" I asked.

"The 'orsenapper!" she said.

"Oh, right," I said.

Della went on dramatically, "A dark shadow fell over me. Before I could turn around to see 'oo it was, 'e clamped a funny-smelling rag over me face. When I came to, I was alone." Della sniffled. "I miss the way 'e nuzzled me, so friendly-like."

"The horsenapper?" I asked.

"The 'orse!"

"Oh, right," I said.

After hearing Della's story, I had a pretty good idea what had 'appened—I mean, happened. But I needed to make a model to be sure.

Using heavy paper and scissors, I quickly cut out two paper dolls, one for Della and one for the horsenapper. I placed Della facing a lamp, with the horsenapper behind her.

Then I turned on the lamp.

Aha!

"Della said the sun was in her eyes."
I pointed at the lamp. "She also said the
horsenapper's shadow fell over her as he
sneaked up on her from behind." I pointed at
the paper dolls.

"But, as you can see, if he was facing the
sun, the horsenapper's shadow would fall
behind him, not in front of him. So Della
couldn't have seen his shadow. In fact," I
announced, "there was no horsenapper. Della
made the whole story up!"

Caught in her lie, Della confessed: a rival
racehorse owner had paid her to hide Bob
until after the Royal Cup.

I 'ope she's 'appy in her prison cell.

Milo frowned. "We can't use a model to catch our suspect in a lie," he said. "We haven't even got a suspect yet."

"First, we need to figure out how money disappeared from a locked box," Jazz said.

"Maybe the thief picked the lock?" Milo suggested. Thieves were always

picking locks in the stories he read in *Whodunnit* magazine.

"It's possible," Jazz said doubtfully.

Milo wished they had the lock there to examine. But the principal had put the empty cashbox in his office till the trial. And the school was closed.

On the other hand . . .

He looked down at the new lesson. What would Dash do?

"Come on," Milo said, standing up. "Let's go."

"Go where?" Jazz asked.

He smiled. "The place that has exactly what we need."

CHAPTER FOUR

"The hardware store?" Jazz asked.

Milo stood proudly in front of the window full of paint supplies and power tools. "We're going to make a model."

"Of what?"

"The locked box."

Jazz lifted an eyebrow. "What what? A hammer and a toilet seat?"

Milo laughed. "We're going to *buy* a cashbox and a lock just like the real ones. If we can figure out how to break into it, we can prove you're not the only one who could have taken the money."

Jazz brightened. "Good idea!"

Inside, they found a metal cashbox exactly like the one at school. Milo spotted a display of locks nearby.

Jazz picked up a small brass padlock. "This is the kind that's on the cashbox."

Milo took it from her. Two tiny keys hung from the lock. They looked just like the key on Jazz's string. Hmm . . .

"Can I help you?" the man behind the counter asked.

Milo held up the padlock and keys. "Do these keys only open up this lock?"

"What else are they supposed to do?" the man asked. "Sing and dance?"

"No, I mean— suppose I had another lock just like this, but I lost the keys. Could I use *these* keys on *that* lock?"

"Sorry," the man said. "Those locks all look the same, but they're not. Only one set of keys fits each lock."

So the lock at school could only have been opened using one of the two keys it came with, Milo thought.

Or, of course—

"How about picking it?" he asked.

The man gave him a sharp glance. "Picking it?"

"If we lost the key," Jazz said hastily, elbowing Milo. "Could we open the lock with a paper clip or something?"

"A *paper clip*?" The man looked offended. "This is a good lock for the price. Now, if you want to saw it off . . ."

Milo laid the padlock on the counter, along with the cashbox they had chosen. "That's okay. We'll just buy a new one."

As the man rang up their order, he asked, "Lose keys a lot? I can make you extras in case you lose these too."

"You can?" Jazz asked.

The man jerked his thumb toward

a sign that said WE COPY KEYS. "As
many as you want. Lowest price in
town." He laughed. "That's a joke. We're
the only place in town that copies keys."

Milo and Jazz exchanged a glance.

"Do you do a lot of those?" Jazz said. "Padlock keys, I mean?"

Milo knew what she was thinking. Omar's key had been home with him all week—but what about *before* this week? Had the thief sneaked off with Omar's key and made a copy?

But the hardware man shook his head. "Can't remember the last time anyone brought one in. Two's usually enough. And padlocks are cheap to replace."

Not *that* cheap, Milo thought as they handed over a month's allowance for the cashbox and the lock.

As they left the hardware store, Jazz said, "It sounds like nobody could have opened that locked box without the key.

I'm almost starting to believe I did it!"

Something was nagging at Milo. Something that the hardware man had said. But what?

Pushing the thought aside, he patted Jazz's shoulder.

"Somebody broke into that cashbox," he said. "So we know it can be done. And I'm going to find out how."

CHAPTER FIVE

Milo rubbed his hands over his face and tried to focus on what his teacher was saying. He couldn't stop yawning. He'd stayed up late trying everything he could think of to break into their locked box. He'd even tried the paper clip.

But he couldn't do it. At least, not without smashing the lock, knocking off the latch, or wrecking the whole box.

And none of those things had happened to the box that had held the money.

Hoping he'd think of something during school, Milo had brought the model cashbox in and stashed it in his desk. But he hadn't gotten any new ideas. And every time he looked at it, he felt more frustrated. *Somebody* knew how to open it without a key. That somebody just wasn't him.

Hmm . . .

Maybe he was doing this all wrong. What he needed was expert help!

As soon as he had free time, he slipped to the computer at the back of the room. He typed in *lock picking* and scanned the search results.

Bingo!

"There's only one possible answer," Milo told Jazz when they met at recess to walk to the trial. "Sneek!"

Jazz looked confused. "Huh?"

"S-N-E-E-K," Milo spelled out. "It's a Dutch town where they hold the world lock-picking championship."

"There's a championship for that?" Jazz asked.

He nodded. "I found it online."

"Don't they all get arrested?"

"No, they just do it as a hobby. They're not allowed to pick anyone else's lock without permission."

Jazz frowned. "What are you saying? You think someone at our school is a secret lock-picking champion?"

"Hey, you never know," Milo said. "We've got kids with skills. What about that second grader who can burp the whole alphabet song?"

Jazz stopped and looked at him. "Is that what you're going to tell the jury?"

Milo grinned. "No. But I learned something else about lock picking. Something I *do* want to tell the jury."

"What?" she asked.

"I found out that it's easy to tell if a lock's been picked. No matter how good someone is at picking locks, they always leave scratches or dents."

Jazz lit up. "So if the lock has marks,

that shows the thief didn't use a key!"

"Which means anybody could have done it," Milo agreed. "Not just you."

He couldn't hold in the grin that spread across his face. Once he proved the lock was picked, the trial would be over. There might even be time for a game of foursquare before recess ended.

As they rounded the corner to the classroom where the trial would be held, a buzz of voices spilled out into the hall.

"I heard she used the money to buy her pet pig a solid gold tiara!"

Jazz froze.

"A diamond collar is what I heard. Maybe the tiara was for *her*."

"That's silly," someone else said. "Jazz doesn't wear stuff like that. Anyway, it was her idea to raise money for the garden in the first place."

"I bet she planned it all along!"

The sound of Chelsea's voice seemed to make Jazz's feet come unstuck from the hallway floor. She marched into the classroom, head held high.

As Milo followed her in, Chelsea was telling everyone, "Now that I'm going to be president—"

"What do you mean, you're going to be president?" Jazz demanded.

The room fell silent.

Folding her arms, Chelsea faced Jazz. "That's what happens when a president's a crook. The president gets kicked out, and the vice president is the new president."

"*I am not a crook!*" Jazz said.

Chelsea and Jazz glared at each other.

Just then, the principal came in with an older girl. The girl was carrying the locked cashbox and a wooden gavel. Milo realized she must be the judge.

The principal sat down at the back of the room. The girl walked to the front, set the cashbox on the desk, and brought her gavel down.

BAM! BAM! BAM!

"Court is in session," she announced.

The students scrambled for seats. Milo moved toward the cashbox, but the judge pointed her gavel and said, "Sit!" He sat.

Before starting the trial, the judge chose the jury by picking twelve names out of a bag. The jury members took their places to the side.

The judge scanned the front of the classroom. "Where is the defendant?"

Jazz raised her hand.

"You are charged with stealing more than a hundred dollars of school garden money from this cashbox," the judge announced. "How do you plead?"

Milo stood. "My client pleads not guilty, your honor."

The judge explained that each side would make a short opening statement. Since Chelsea, as prosecutor, had to show that Jazz was guilty, she'd go first.

Chelsea rose and turned to the jury.

"It's obvious Jazz did it. Everybody heard her say she was the only one at school who had the key." She sat down, looking smug.

"Defense?" the judge said.

Milo stood.

"Jazz *was* the only one with a key," he said. "But the thief didn't need a key. The lock was picked—and I can prove it." He pointed at the cashbox on the desk. "May I, your honor?"

The judge nodded.

Every eye in the room was on Milo as he peered at the dangling padlock.

It didn't have a single scratch.

CHAPTER SIX

Milo stared at the undamaged lock.

The judge leaned over for a look. "What do you see?"

"N-n-nothing," Milo stammered. "But—but—that's impossible!"

He turned the padlock over, but there were no scratches or dents.

Finally, the judge asked if he had anything else to say in Jazz's defense. Miserably, Milo shook his head. As he slunk back to his seat, he saw the jury members whispering to each other.

"Thanks anyway," Jazz said. "It was a good idea."

It was more than just a good idea, Milo thought stubbornly. The lock *must* have been picked. How else could the money disappear from the locked box? Magic? This was Westview Elementary, not Hogwarts!

The trial continued. Chelsea called Billy to the witness stand. He bounded to the front of the room, beaming.

"It was your idea to put Jazz on trial," Chelsea said. "Right?"

Billy nodded.

"So you think she stole the money."

He looked confused. "I never said . . ."

"Did you say anybody else should be put on trial?" Chelsea pressed.

"Well, no," Billy admitted. "But—"

"Jazz even said she was the only one who could have opened the cashbox. Didn't she?"

"I don't think she meant—"

"Answer the question!" Chelsea snapped. "Did you hear her say that?"

Billy looked unhappy. "I guess I did."

Chelsea smiled. "I rest my case."

When the judge asked Milo if he had any questions for the witness, Milo said, "Billy, you know Jazz. Is she honest?"

"Sure!" Billy said. Then he hesitated. "I mean . . . I always thought so, anyway."

Murmurs came from the jury.

As Billy stepped down, he tossed Jazz an apologetic look.

"Do you have any other witnesses?" the judge asked Chelsea.

Smirking, Chelsea shook her head.

The judge turned to Milo. "Your turn, then."

Milo's mind raced. His whole plan for the trial had been to clear Jazz's name by proving that a thief had picked the lock. Instead, he had made her look guiltier than ever.

Now what?

Everybody in the school knew Jazz. And everybody—*almost* everybody— liked her. If she said she was innocent, the jury members would believe her. Wouldn't they?

He stood. "Your honor, I call Jazz."

Jazz raised her hand and promised to tell the truth, the whole truth, and nothing but the truth. Then she sat in the witness chair beside the judge and gazed

around the room.

Answering Milo's questions, she described everything that had happened, from putting away the locked cashbox full of money to opening it the next day and finding it empty.

"Were you surprised?" Milo asked.

"Of course I was surprised," she said. "I was totally shocked!"

It was time to ask.

"So . . . you didn't steal the money?"

"NO!"

Milo glanced at the jury. Some of them were giving Jazz skeptical looks. Others didn't seem to want to meet her eyes.

"Do you have any more questions?" the judge asked Milo.

He swallowed. "No. That's all."

It was Chelsea's turn to question Jazz.

Yes, Jazz said, she was sure she'd locked the cashbox. Yes, it was still locked the next day. Yes, she and Omar had the only keys.

"And Omar's been home sick," Chelsea said. "Which means that you're the only one who could have sneaked into the office when nobody was around, unlocked the box, and taken the school garden money. Right?" Before Jazz could answer, Chelsea turned to the jury. "It's obvious she did it."

Jazz looked at Chelsea.

"Obvious," Jazz repeated slowly. "You keep saying that. But maybe it's *too* obvious."

"What's that supposed to mean?" Chelsea demanded.

"If I stole the money, why would I lock the cashbox afterward?" Jazz said. "The locked box makes me look guilty. All I had to do was break the lock or take the whole box. Then it would look as if anybody could have done it."

Milo wanted to cheer for his partner. Leave it to Jazz to think like a detective, no matter what!

For an instant, Chelsea looked startled. Then she shrugged and said, "Too bad you didn't think of that *before* you stole the money."

"I didn't do it!" Jazz protested.

Ignoring her, Chelsea faced the jury. "We know nobody picked the lock.

He proved that." She pointed at Milo, who winced.

"And it didn't just unlock itself," Chelsea went on. "Someone unlocked it. Someone with a key. And there's only one person that it could have been."

Bzzzzzzzzzzzzz!

The bell rang for the end of recess. The principal stood and announced that they would finish the trial the next day, and kids began shuffling out.

But Milo didn't move.

Chelsea was right, he thought. There *was* only one person who could have unlocked the box.

And he was sure now who it was.

CHAPTER SEVEN

"You think *Omar* stole the money?" Jazz stopped in the middle of the sidewalk and stared at Milo.

Milo had waited impatiently all afternoon for school to let out so he could tell Jazz his idea.

"*Someone* unlocked that cashbox! And we know it wasn't you. It has to be the only other person with a key."

"But Omar hasn't even been in school this week," Jazz said.

"That's what he wants us to think," Milo said. "But what if he's been faking sick so he could sneak into school and steal the money?"

"Omar? He's so honest!"

"Maybe he's been faking honest, too."

"Milo . . ."

"Can't you see it?" Milo demanded. "The office lady goes out at dismissal time to help the kids get on their buses. Omar zips in. He takes the money, locks the box back up, and zoom—he's out the door, and nobody knows he was there. Easy as pie."

"Somebody would see him going in or out," Jazz said.

"Sure, but they wouldn't notice him with all the other kids milling around. And if they did, he could say he was going to the office to pick up the work he missed."

"What about his family?" Jazz said.

"Wouldn't he get caught leaving the house when he's supposed to be sick?"

"They might have gone out."

Jazz shook her head. "I just can't believe Omar would steal the money. He's super serious about his job as student council treasurer."

"At least we should question him," Milo insisted.

Jazz looked troubled, but agreed.

When they reached Omar's house, though, no one answered the doorbell. Milo pressed the button again and again.

"Nobody's home," Jazz told him. "Let's go."

Disappointed, Milo trailed after her. At the corner, he glanced back. "*Hey!*"

"What?" Jazz asked.

He pointed. "There! At the window! On the second floor!"

Just for a second, he had seen a face. Now it was gone.

"I don't see anything," Jazz said.

Milo ran back and pounded his fist on the door. He waited, but nobody came.

Jazz pulled his sleeve. "Come on."

Frustrated, Milo let her lead him off. He'd seen Omar's face at the window! He was sure of it!

Now Milo was even more convinced of Omar's guilt. Omar must have heard them knocking, but he hadn't answered the door. If he was innocent, why would he hide from them?

Milo knew so far he'd done a terrible job of defending Jazz. But tomorrow he'd do better. He would show the jury Omar *had* to be the thief.

He worked on his speech till bedtime, then again at breakfast the next morning. He left for school so late, he had to  run all the way. He slid into his seat just as the bell rang.

At recess, Jazz met him inside the trial room. He started to tell her about all the work he'd done, but she interrupted.

"Omar's back in school!"

Milo couldn't believe his ears. "Really?"

Jazz nodded. "And—"

"This is GREAT!" Milo cut in.

He would call Omar to the stand. Confront him with his crime. Maybe he could surprise Omar into a confession, the way lawyers always did in trials on TV.

"Listen, Milo—"

He waved Jazz aside. "Not now, okay? I need to—"

"*Milo!* Look!"

He turned.

Into the trial room, surrounded by his friends, came Omar . . . in a wheelchair.

CHAPTER EIGHT

"I tried to tell you," Jazz said. "See? He wasn't faking."

All the kids who hadn't already seen Omar crowded around, asking him what happened.

"Fell out of a tree," Omar explained. "Sprained *both* my ankles, so I can't use crutches. I couldn't even come to school until the wheelchair was delivered!"

Milo's mind reeled.

Omar couldn't possibly be the thief. With two sprained ankles, there was no way he could have sneaked out of his house and walked to school. And he certainly couldn't have dashed into the office and run away with the money.

But if Omar didn't do it . . . who did?

Omar wheeled up to Milo and Jazz. "That was you two at the door yesterday, wasn't it? I heard you knocking, but I knew I'd never get downstairs in time." He grinned. "I have to go bump, bump, bump on my butt."

"That's okay," Jazz said. "We just wanted to talk to you about the trial."

Omar's grin faded. "I know you're not the one who took that money, Jazz. That's not the kind of thing that you would do."

"I'm glad you believe me," Jazz said. "I wish *they* did."

Milo followed her gaze to the jury. What was he going to do? The trial was ending, and he hadn't been able to knock a hole in the case against Jazz. Would she be found guilty while the real thief went free?

The principal came in with the judge from the middle school, who banged her gavel and called the room to order.

The judge explained that each side would get to make a closing statement.

Then the jury would go off to decide whether Chelsea had proved Jazz's guilt.

Milo barely heard the judge's words. His eyes were pinned to the cashbox she had set before her on the desk, and his brain was working furiously.

Omar's key hadn't opened the box. Neither had Jazz's. And the lock hadn't been picked.

So how had more than a hundred dollars disappeared from a locked box?

There had to be some trick—some other way of opening the box. But Milo had spent hours trying to break into the model cashbox, the one they'd gotten from the hardware store.

Where had he gone wrong?

Maybe the problem was their model.

It looked just like the cashbox sitting on the judge's desk—an ordinary cashbox with an ordinary lock. Was there some hidden difference, though?

Like the hardware store man said: those little padlocks might all look the same, but they weren't really the same.

Look the same.

But not the same.

Milo sat bolt upright. That was it!

"Your honor!" He jumped to his feet. "Wait! Stop!"

"What is it?" the judge asked.

"I—I need to go out for a minute," Milo said.

"You should have done that before you came in," she told him.

"No! I don't—I mean—" He gave up. "Never mind! I'll be right back! Please, please, don't finish the trial without me!" Not waiting for an answer, he burst out of the room.

Milo hurtled down the hall, praying he wouldn't get stopped for breaking the No Running rule. He bet he was leaving scorch marks in the hallway!

When he returned, huffing and puffing, Jazz rushed up to him. "Milo!

What's going on?"

Milo bent over, gasping for breath.
"I . . . know . . . who . . . stole . . . the . . .
money."

"What? Who?"

Hands on knees, he looked up at Jazz.
"Who wanted to get you in trouble? Who
wanted to take your place as president?"

"Chelsea?" she gasped.

He nodded. "It was Chelsea all along."

CHAPTER NiNE

Pandemonium.

Chelsea was on her feet. Her mouth moved, but her words couldn't be heard over all the other excited voices.

Bam. Bam. Bam. "Order in the court!" The judge pointed at Chelsea. "Sit."

"But he can't—"

"*Now.*"

Chelsea sat.

The judge turned to Milo. "Explain, please."

"It was the padlocks!" Milo said. "They didn't have to *be* the same at all. They only had to *look* the same."

"What do you mean?" Jazz cut in.

"Remember how Chelsea knocked the worms and dirt on the floor? And I thought she did it so she could steal the money while you were cleaning up?"

Jazz nodded.

"Well, I was right. Or almost right. She didn't take the money then. But she took something else: the lock."

"Huh?" Jazz said. "But the lock was still on the box at the end of lunch that day. I locked it myself."

"You locked *a* lock," Milo told her. "But it was Chelsea's lock, not yours."

Jazz frowned. "No, that's impossible.

The next day I unlocked it again—with my own key."

Milo glanced around the room. Everyone looked as confused as Jazz, except for Chelsea, who looked sick.

He turned to the jury.

"Okay, let's go back to the beginning. Chelsea's at the snack table with Jazz. The cashbox is sitting open on the table. The open lock is hanging from the box."

Milo walked over to the cashbox. "Can I use this?" he asked.

The judge nodded.

Milo held his hand out to Jazz. "Key, please."

Jazz slipped the string over her head and handed it to him. He unlocked the padlock, flipped the cashbox lid open, and left the open padlock dangling.

"With me so far?" he asked the jury.

A few nods.

Milo went on. "Chelsea 'accidentally' knocks a cup off the table and makes a big mess, which Jazz has to clean up. While Jazz is down on the floor, Chelsea pulls the switch."

Milo reached for his jacket pocket, and then stopped. "Does anybody have a pair of gloves?"

A girl handed him a pair of pink
gloves with white snowflakes. Ignoring
the snickers, Milo put them on, then
pulled a small padlock from his pocket.
He held it up so everyone could see.

"Chelsea takes the lock off the box.
Then she puts her own lock on."

He took the lock from the cashbox,
hanging the new lock in its place.

"As you can see," he told the jury, "it's the same kind of lock. It looks just like the other one, so Jazz doesn't notice the switch."

Murmurs from the jury.

"At the end of lunch, Jazz locks the cashbox up—" He snapped the lock shut. *Click.* "—and takes it to the office, just like always."

He glanced at Jazz. Her bright eyes told him she had caught on.

"Later, when no one's in the office, Chelsea sneaks in and unlocks her lock." Milo pulled out a little key, opened the new lock, and dropped it on the table. "She takes the money. Then she switches locks again." He put the first lock back on and shut it. *Click.*

"So when Jazz goes to open the box—"

"It's locked, but the money is gone," Jazz finished for him. "And it looks as if no one could have taken it but me."

For a moment, no one spoke.

"Can you prove it?" the judge asked.

Still wearing the gloves, Milo picked up the lock he had taken from his pocket. "I'm sure the police can check this for Chelsea's fingerprints."

Chelsea let out an angry shriek.

"You had no right to go digging in my backpack—" She clapped a hand over her mouth.

Milo grinned at the judge.

"How's that for proof?" he asked. "Your Honor?"

For the first time, the judge smiled.

"I'd say it's pretty good."

CHAPTER TEN

Milo handed Omar a dollar and took a packet of sunflower seeds and a napkin folded into the shape of a watering can. Omar put the dollar in the cashbox.

"Not much money in there now," Milo said.

"Omar and I decided it was safer to leave most of it with the office lady," Jazz said. "We only keep enough in the cashbox to make change."

"How much have you earned so far?" Milo asked.

"About a hundred and fifty bucks! Counting the hundred Chelsea stole."

Chelsea had given back the money. The principal offered her a student trial, but she begged him to just choose her punishment himself.

Chelsea had to write an apology to Jazz—and read it aloud over the school PA. She also was suspended for a week.

 When she came back, she'd miss recess for two more weeks while she helped dig the new school garden.

Of course, she also lost her position as student council vice president. And she wouldn't be allowed to run for president the next year.

"Who's going to be the new veepee?" Milo asked.

"Me!" Billy came up to the table, beaming even more brightly than usual. "That's what happens when the vice president turns out to be a crook."

They all laughed.

"Now we'll need a new secretary."
Jazz poked Milo. "Interested?"

He shook his head. "I'm too busy with
trials."

Everyone but Chelsea loved the new
student court. And Milo was the most
popular lawyer in school.

"Not too busy for sleuthing, though,"
Jazz said. "Right, partner?"

Milo dug out his detective notebook.
"I was just figuring out what to tell Dash

about The Case of the Locked Box."

"I've been wondering," Omar said. "When you went running off during the trial, you weren't gone that long. How did you find Chelsea's lock so fast?"

Milo and Jazz exchanged a glance.

"I didn't," Milo said.

Omar's eyes widened. "But we saw it. And you said—the fingerprints—"

Milo grinned. "I said the police could check for Chelsea's fingerprints. I didn't say they'd find them!"

"Milo and I bought that lock at the hardware store." Jazz explained about the model cashbox, then went on, "The lock was on the cashbox in Milo's desk. When he realized what Chelsea had done, he ran and got it."

"I figured Chelsea wouldn't be able to tell it wasn't hers," Milo continued. "After all—"

Jazz finished the sentence with him.
"All these locks look the same!"

SUPER SLEUTHING STRATEGIES

A few days after Milo and Jazz wrote to Dash Marlowe, a letter arrived in the mail. . . .

Greetings, Milo and Jazz,

Congratulations! This case was one for the record books. Milo, very few detectives have argued a case in court— and won! And Jazz, even fewer have wound up as defendants! Of course, I was once falsely accused of faking evidence—by a jealous rival sleuth. My blood still boils when I think of The Case of the Dirty Detective. . . .

Happy Sleuthing!
—*Dash Marlowe*

Warm Up!

Here are some brain stretchers to keep you fit to foil the cleverest culprits! If you have any doubts about your answers, take a look at the last page of this letter.

1. How can you make seven an even number?
2. The barber shop in your town has two barbers. One has a nice, neatly trimmed head of hair. The other's hair is a mess. Which barber should you use?
3. What happens once in a minute, twice in a moment, and not even once in a hundred years?
4. The more it dries, the wetter it gets. What is it?

Hello, Burglar! Come On In! An Observation Puzzle

Your mystery reminded me of a building I once came across. What careless tenants! Only *one* worried about robberies. The rest left doors and windows open—and keys in obvious places! See if you can spot all the careless things the tenants did. (Hint: There are six.)

Answer: Windows are open in 1B and 3A; doors in 2A, 1B. And see the keys by 1A's mat and 2B's windowsill? 3B is the only place a burglar would skip!

A Robber's Guide to Theft Prevention: A Logic Puzzle

Three ex-robbers always worried about . . . robbers!
Each had a special item he wanted to keep safe and his
own idea of how to do that. Try to figure out what item
each guy treasured and how he protected it.

Look at the clues and fill in the answer box where
you can. Then read the clues again to find the answer.

Answer Box *(see answers on next page)*

	Rocky	Louie	Sal
Treasure			
How protected			

1. Rocky loved the clown mask he wore on his first
   bank holdup.
2. The ex-robber who adored his rubber ducky put it
   in a box, hung it from a canoe, and put the canoe in
   a lake.
3. Louie hid his treasure in his cat's litter box.
4. One guy hid his most beloved item in a package in
   the freezer labeled "Lasagna."
5. One ex-robber prized his first Wanted poster and
   meant to keep it forever.

Stolen at Sea: A Mini-Mystery

Check this out and draw your own conclusion!

It was a dark and stormy night—really. I wouldn't have minded except that I was on a ship and more than a little queasy. I was wishing something would distract me from the rolling and lurching when the captain called me. Sometime during the last half hour a fortune in jewels had been stolen from the safe in a film star's state room.

Only two people knew where the jewels had been kept: the star's assistant, Frank Beck, and her maid, Mabel Drudge. Beck told me he'd been alone in his cabin writing notes. He showed me several different ones, each of which began in neat, precise block letters, "I'm having a pleasant trip but missing you a lot." The maid, pointing to headphones and a music player, said she'd been alone in her cabin listening to the soundtrack from *The Little Mermaid*. I knew right away that one of them was lying. Who was it?

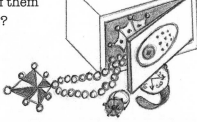

Answer: Beck. There was no way he could have produced such neat, perfect writing while the ship tossed in the savage storm.

Answer to Logic Puzzle: Sal kept his beloved rubber ducky in a box hung from a canoe in a lake. He often took it out for a swim. Rocky kept the mask he wore on his first bank holdup in his freezer in a package labeled "Lasagna." Louie hid his first Wanted poster in a plastic bag in his cat's litter box. (I know—ewww.)

105

EEEEK! A Make-a-Model Story

Making a model has saved me grief in more than one case. There's nothing better for helping clients understand how something works! Here's one story.

A desperate client came to me wringing his hands and crying, "There's a giant monster in my basement!" He'd gone down there to turn off a light, but when he saw a huge shadow of an eight-legged creature on his wall, he flew back upstairs. Too afraid to return to the basement on his own, he begged me to investigate. When I searched, all I found was a small rubber spider that belonged to his young son.

I guessed right away what had happened, but my client refused to believe me. So, using a flashlight and the rubber spider, I recreated his "giant shadow monster" on the kitchen wall. How did I do it? (Hint: If you're not sure, try making a model yourself with a flashlight and any small object.)

Answer: I asked my client to hold up the rubber spider several feet away from the kitchen wall. Then I shined my flashlight on the spider. The closer the flashlight got to the spider, the bigger the shadow on the wall grew—until it really did look like a monster's shadow! (Try it for yourself and see what kind of giant shadow creatures you can create.)

Answers to Brain Stretchers:
1. Take out the *s*.
2. Since there are only two barbers in town, they must each cut each other's hair. So you should go to the barber with the bad haircut.
3. The letter *m*.
4. A towel.

★ *Booklist* **STARRED REVIEW** and
Book Links' Best New Books for the Classroom
for *The Case of the Stinky Socks*

Moonbeam Children's Book Awards
The Case of the July 4ᵗʰ Jinx: Silver Medalist
The Case of the Superstar Scam: Bronze Medalist
The Case of the Buried Bones: Silver Medalist

Silver Falchion Award for Best Children's Chapter Book
The Case of the Locked Box

Titles in *The Milo & Jazz Mysteries* series:

The Case of the Stinky Socks
The Case of the Poisoned Pig
The Case of the *Haunted* Haunted House
The Case of the Amazing Zelda
The Case of the July 4ᵗʰ Jinx
The Case of the Missing Moose
The Case of the Purple Pool
The Case of the Diamonds in the Desk
The Case of the Crooked Campaign
The Case of the Superstar Scam
The Case of the Locked Box
The Case of the Buried Bones

Visit **www.kanepress.com** for
Detective's Guides and more!

#6: The Case of the Missing Moose

"Engaging . . . Fun pen-and-ink illustrations enhance the story. Numerous clues are provided . . . and the mystery has a surprising twist at the end." —*Booklist*

#7: The Case of the Purple Pool

"Young readers might just have to exercise their brains to solve this one. I think mystery fans ages 6–10 will enjoy this series." —Semicolon blog

#8: The Case of the Diamonds in the Desk

"Sprightly illustrations enliven the brief chapters, which are filled with earnest, clever kids being funny—and, more importantly, smart." —*Booklist*

#9: The Case of the Crooked Campaign

"A hilarious circus of clues . . . Kids will have a fantastic time keeping up with the sleuthing action." —*Midwest Book Review*

#10: The Case of the Superstar Scam

2011 Moonbeam Children's Book Award Bronze Medalist
"Lots of fun." —*Booklist*

#11: The Case of the Locked Box

"A superior entry in this early chapter mystery series . . . A combination mystery/legal thriller, this is one book that will have its young readers guessing both whodunit and howdunit right up to the very end. Highly recommended." —*Mysterious Reviews, Hidden Staircase Mysteries*

#12: The Case of the Buried Bones

"Milo and Jazz return to solve their twelfth mystery, and they do so with style. Clever and fun." —*Booklist*

Visit **www.kanepress.com** to see all titles in The Milo & Jazz Mysteries.

Make It Work

(Grades K–3 • Ages 5–8)
"Easy-to-read stories with plenty of opportunity for problem-solving and hands-on action. Highly recommended."
—*Children's Bookwatch*

Math Matters®

(Grades K–3 • Ages 5–8)
Winner of a *Learning* Magazine Teachers' Choice Award

"These cheerfully illustrated titles offer primary-grade children practice in math as well as reading."—*Booklist*

(Grades PreK & Up • Ages 4 & Up)
"A cheerful addition to the growing list of math-related picture books."—*Booklist* (for *The Mousier the Merrier!*)

(Grades K–3 • Ages 5–8)
"A wonderful tool for the teacher who wants to integrate reading and science."—*National Science Teachers Association*

SOCIAL STUDIES CONNECTS®

(Grades K–3 • Ages 5–8)
"This series is very strongly recommended..."
—*Children's Bookwatch*

ABOUT THE AUTHOR

Lewis B. Montgomery is the pen name of a writer whose favorite authors include CSL, EBW, and LMM. Those initials are a clue—but there's another clue, too. Can you figure out their names?

Besides writing the Milo & Jazz mysteries, LBM enjoys eating spicy Thai noodles and blueberry ice cream, riding a bike, and reading. Not all at the same time, of course. At least, not anymore. But that's another story. . . .

ABOUT THE ILLUSTRATOR

Amy Wummer has illustrated more than 50 children's books. She uses pencils, watercolors, and ink—but not the invisible kind.

Amy and her husband, who is also an artist, live in Pennsylvania . . . in a mysterious old house which has a secret hidden room in the basement!